The Maze

Level 4A

Written by Deborah Chancellor
Illustrated by Monica Armino

What is synthetic phonics?

Synthetic phonics teaches children to recognise the sounds of letters and to blend (synthesise) them together to make whole words.

Understanding sound/letter relationships gives children the confidence and ability to read unfamiliar words, without having to rely on memory or guesswork; this helps them to progress towards independent reading.

Did you know? Spoken English uses more than 40 speech sounds. Each sound is called a *phoneme*. Some phonemes relate to a single letter (d-o-g) and others to combinations of letters (sh-ar-p). When a phoneme is written down it is called a *grapheme*. Teaching these sounds, matching them to their written form and sounding out words for reading is the basis of synthetic phonics.

Consultant

I love reading phonics has been created in consultation with language expert Abigail Steel. She has a background in teaching and teacher training and is a respected expert in the field of synthetic phonics. Abigail Steel is a regular contributor to educational publications. Her international education consultancy supports parents and teachers in the promotion of literacy skills.

Reading tips

This book focuses on the ai sound, made with the letter formation a-e, as in game.

Tricky words in this book

Any words in bold may have unusual spellings or are new and have not yet been introduced.

> Tricky words in this book:
>
> **wow want face give race**

Extra ways to have fun with this book

After the reader has read the story, ask them questions about what they have just read:

Did you learn any new words in the book?
Which page was your favourite and why?

This way to the AMAZING maze!

A pronunciation guide

This grid contains the sounds used in the stories in levels 4, 5 and 6 and a guide on how to say them. /**a**/ represents the sounds made, rather than the letters in a word.

/**ai**/ as in game	/**ai**/ as in play/they	/**ee**/ as in leaf/these	/**ee**/ as in he
/**igh**/ as in kite/light	/**igh**/ as in find/sky	/**oa**/ as in home	/**oa**/ as in snow
/**oa**/ as in cold	/**y+oo**/ as in cube/music/new	long /**oo**/ as in flute/crew/blue	/**oi**/ as in boy
/**er**/ as in bird/hurt	/**or**/ as in snore/oar/door	/**or**/ as in dawn/sauce/walk	/**e**/ as in head
/**e**/ as in said/any	/**ou**/ as in cow	/**u**/ as in touch	/**air**/ as in hare/bear/there
/**eer**/ as in deer/here/cashier	/**t**/ as in tripped/skipped	/**d**/ as in rained	/**j**/ as in gent/gin/gym
/**j**/ as in barge/hedge	/**s**/ as in cent/circus/cyst	/**s**/ as in prince	/**s**/ as in house
/**ch**/ as in itch/catch	/**w**/ as in white	/**h**/ as in who	/**r**/ as in write/rhino

Sounds in this story are
highlighted in the grid.

/**f**/ as in phone	/**f**/ as in rough	/**ul**/ as in pencil/ hospital	/**z**/ as in fries/ cheese/breeze
/**n**/ as in knot/ gnome/engine	/**m**/ as in welcome /thumb/column	/**g**/ as in guitar/ghost	/**zh**/ as in vision/beige
/**k**/ as in chord	/**k**/ as in plaque/ bouquet	/**nk**/ as in uncle	/**ks**/ as in box/books/ ducks/cakes
/**a**/ and /**o**/ as in hat/what	/**e**/ and /**ee**/ as in bed/he	/**i**/ and /**igh**/ as in fin/find	/**o**/ and /**oa**/ as in hot/cold
/**u**/ and short /**oo**/ as in but/put	/**ee**/, /**e**/ and /**ai**/ as in eat/ bread/break	/**igh**/, /**ee**/ and /**e**/ as in tie/field/friend	/**ou**/ and /**oa**/ as in cow/blow
/**ou**/, /**oa**/ and /**oo**/ as in out/ shoulder/could	/**i**/ and /**ai**/ as in money/they	/**c**/ and /**s**/ as in cat/cent	/**y**/, /**igh**/ and /**i**/ as in yes/sky/myth
/**g**/ and /**j**/ as in got/giant	/**ch**/, /**c**/ and / **sh**/ as in chin/ school/chef	/**er**/, /**air**/ and /**eer**/ as in earth/bear/ears	/**u**/, /**ou**/ and /**oa**/ as in plough/dough

Be careful not to add an 'uh' sound to 's', 't', 'p',
'c', 'h', 'r', 'm', 'd', 'g', 'l', 'f' and 'b'. For example,
say 'fff' not 'fuh' and 'sss' not 'suh'.

Jake and Jane see a maze.
"**Wow**!" Jake says.
"I **want** to go in!"

Jane makes a **face**.
"I don't like mazes."

Jake takes a cake out of his bag.
"If you go in the maze, you can
have this cake," Jake says.

Jake runs off into the maze.
He waves the cake at Jane.
"Come on!" he says.

Jane chases after Jake.

"I want cake!" she cries.

Jake and Jane get lost in
the maze. They are stuck in the
maze for a long time.

"I **give** up!" says Jake.
Jane's tummy starts to rumble.
Jake's does too.

"Can we have the cake now?"
she asks.

The cake is very good.
Jake and Jane cheer up.
"Let's have a **race**!" Jake says.

Jake and Jane race round
the maze.

Will Jane find the way out?
Will Jake find it first?

"I won!" Jane shouts.
"I like mazes!"

OVER 48 TITLES IN SIX LEVELS
Abigail Steel recommends...

Other titles to enjoy from Level 4

The Maze
978-1-84898-559-9

Fairy Fay's Bad Day
978-1-84898-560-5

Pirate School
978-1-84898-566-7

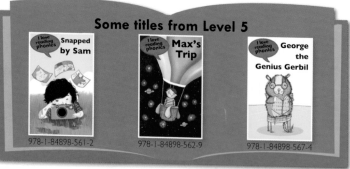

Some titles from Level 5

Snapped by Sam
978-1-84898-561-2

Max's Trip
978-1-84898-562-9

George the Genius Gerbil
978-1-84898-567-4

Some titles from Level 6

What Wally Wanted
978-1-84898-563-6

Superhero Ed
978-1-84898-564-3

The Robot Bop
978-1-84898-570-4

An Hachette UK Company
www.hachette.co.uk

Copyright © Octopus Publishing Group Ltd 2012
First published in Great Britain in 2012 by TickTock, an imprint of Octopus Publishing Group Ltd,
Endeavour House, 189 Shaftesbury Avenue, London WC2H 8JY.
www.octopusbooks.co.uk

ISBN 978 1 84898 559 9

Printed and bound in China
10 9 8 7 6 5 4 3 2 1